HOW TO TAKE YOUR
Grandmother
TO THE
Museum

by Lois Wyse
and Molly Rose Goldman

illustrated by Marie-Louise Gay

An American Museum of Natural History Book

City & Company

Workman Publishing • New York

Library of Congress Cataloging-in-Publication Data

Wyse, Lois.
  How to take your grandmother to the museum / by Lois Wyse and Molly Rose Goldman; illustrated by Marie-Louise Gay.

     p.   cm.

     ISBN 0-7611-0990-0
     [1. Natural history museums—Fiction. 2. Museums—Fiction. 3. Grandmothers—Fiction.] I. Gay, Marie-Louise, ill. II. Title. PZ7.W994Ho   1998
[E]—dc21   98-7707
                                                            CIP
                                                            AC

All photographs courtesy the American Museum of Natural History, except p. 34 © Schecter Lee and p. 38 © Vincent Perez/Anatomyworks.

Cover and interior design by Nancy Loggins Gonzalez

Published by
Workman Publishing Company, Inc.
708 Broadway
New York, New York 10003-9555

Manufactured in Singapore
First printing September 1998
10 9 8 7 6 5 4 3 2

Molly dedicates this book to her parents
Katherine Wyse Goldman and Henry Goldman
and to her big brother Max.

Lois dedicates this book to all of The Cousins
(Marisa, Elizabeth, Sarah Guber; Stephanie,
Alex, Emily Wyse; and Max Goldman)
because each one of them has opened
her eyes in new ways to the museum of life.

I've known my grandmother all my life, and she's taken me to lots of Interesting Places. We went to an art gallery to look at paintings and to a theater to see a play. We went to a planetarium to see stars I'd never seen before. My grandmother and I have never been to an Interesting Place that she hadn't been to before.

Then one day our class went to visit the Museum of Natural History. It was a great trip, and I told my grandma all about it. "My favorite dinosaur is *Tyrannosaurus rex*," I said. "What's your favorite, Grandma?"

Grandma thought for a moment. "I don't remember ever seeing a dinosaur up close," she said. "I guess that's because I've never been to the Museum of Natural History."

"Never, Grandma?" I was more than surprised. I was shocked. But I didn't say so.

That night, lying in bed counting the glow-in-the-dark dinosaur stickers on my ceiling, I had an idea.

6

Early the next morning I called my grandmother. "Grandma," I said. "This is me. I want to take you to an Interesting Place."

"You do?" She sounded as surprised as when my aunt had twins.

"I want to take you to the Museum of Natural History."

"Why, thank you," said Grandma. "That will be a real treat."

"We'll be doing a lot of walking," I
told her, "so remember to wear comfortable
shoes. And make sure you go to the bathroom before
you leave home. They do have bathrooms there, but a grandmother could get lost looking for one."

Saturday morning, as we climbed the steps of the museum, I saw that Grandma had taken my advice about the shoes. So I gave her a little more advice. "Stay close to me at all times," I told her, "and do *not* wander off by yourself."

"I won't," she promised. "Now, where do we begin?"

"With the dinosaurs," I told her.

I had a feeling Grandma would like dinosaurs, maybe because they are even older than she is.

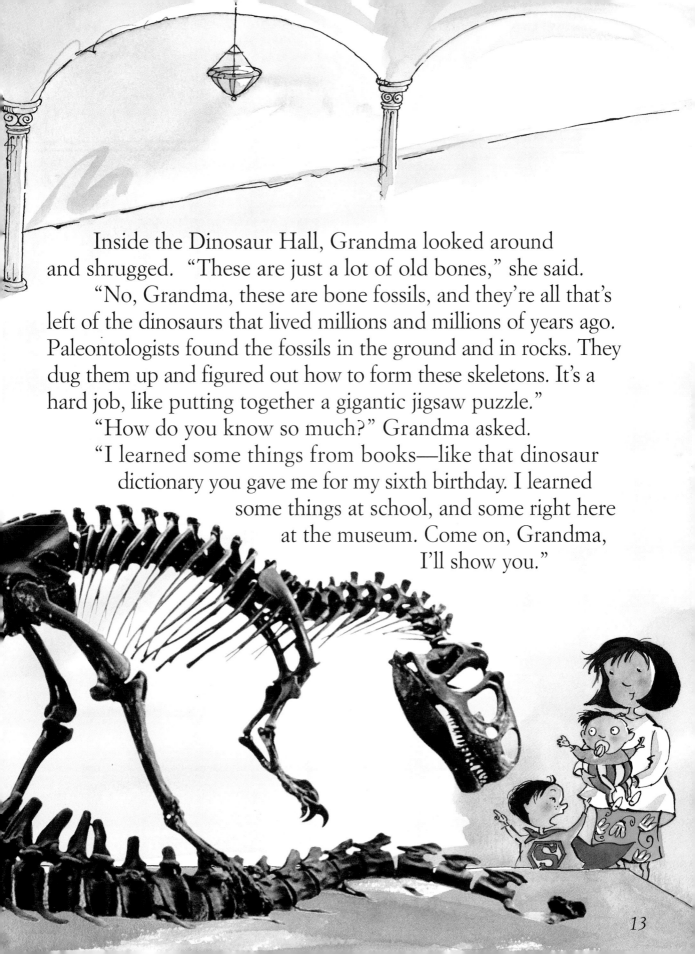

Inside the Dinosaur Hall, Grandma looked around and shrugged. "These are just a lot of old bones," she said.

"No, Grandma, these are bone fossils, and they're all that's left of the dinosaurs that lived millions and millions of years ago. Paleontologists found the fossils in the ground and in rocks. They dug them up and figured out how to form these skeletons. It's a hard job, like putting together a gigantic jigsaw puzzle."

"How do you know so much?" Grandma asked.

"I learned some things from books—like that dinosaur dictionary you gave me for my sixth birthday. I learned some things at school, and some right here at the museum. Come on, Grandma, I'll show you."

We saw *Anatotitan*, whose mouth was shaped like a duck's bill. Grandma put on her glasses and together we read about *Stegosaurus*. I showed her the bony plates running down its back. They looked just like little sails on a ship.

Then I pointed to the ceiling, where the fossils of two pterosaurs hung.

"Pterosaurs are flying reptiles," I told Grandma. "*Tupuxuara* had a wingspan of 8 feet, but *Pteranodon* was even bigger. It had a wingspan of 23 feet."

"Unbelievable," said Grandma. "Imagine one of them stopping at my bird feeder!"

Together we walked under the long, long tail of *Apatosaurus*, one of my favorite plant-eaters of all time.

Finally we saw *Tyrannosaurus rex* towering over us. Grandma and I looked up at its 5-foot-long head and its gigantic open mouth. Together we counted its 60 razor-sharp teeth.

"Those teeth look like giant steak knives," Grandma said.
We read how *T. rex* walked on its toes, the same way a bird does.
"Did you know that?" Grandma asked.

I admitted that I did. "I guess you're doing what you always tell me to do, Grandma—learn one new thing every day."

"One thing?" Grandma laughed. "I think I've already learned at least *ten* new things. But I'm all set to learn more. What's next?"

"We're going on a little trip."

Grandma's eyes got very wide. "Where?" she asked.

"To Africa," I said. "Follow me!" We took a shortcut through Asia and turned left at Central America. Soon we were surrounded by antelopes and monkeys and cheetahs.

Grandma was so amazed she wasn't sure where to look first.

It's a good thing I was there to be her guide.

"This feels like a safari," she said.

"They're all real animals, not paintings," I explained. "These kinds of exhibits are called dioramas."

"The antelopes are looking at us," Grandma whispered.

"And I can almost hear the gorilla thumping its chest," I said.

Grandma stopped to see the ostriches. "I once had a hat with an ostrich plume," she said.

"Grandma! Did you kill a bird for one of its feathers?"

"*I* didn't, but somebody did. We don't do that anymore."

I breathed a sigh of relief. "Good," I said. "We have to save our wildlife."

As we were leaving Africa, Grandma asked, "Where next?"

Oh, that Grandma, there's no stopping her once she gets going!

"How about an Arctic expedition?" I suggested.

"I'll have to get ready for that," Grandma said.

Just then I remembered that a grandma can get tired on a
long trip, so I found a nice bench for her to sit on. "You can rest
as long as you want."

"Rest? Who needs a rest?" she said. "I'm just stopping to
get my thermal-lined hiking boots."

Grandma reached into her bag and pretended to pull out two pairs of hiking boots. "I brought a pair for you too," she said. "Sit down next to me and we'll put them on together."

We laced up our boots and then, hand in hand, we began to trek across the icy landscape. Up ahead was a snow-covered mountain. On our way to the top we saw a family of mountain goats and two huge Alaskan brown bears.

"You were right about dioramas making you feel as if

you're really making the trip," Grandma said. "Why, this seems
so real that I even feel the change in altitude. You know the air
gets thinner the higher up you go."

"Then maybe it's time to go down," I said. "Way down . . .
to the bottom of the ocean."

"I never knew there were so many places to travel inside
one museum," Grandma said as she caught her breath.

"This is the Hall of
Ocean Life," I explained.
"Some life," Grandma said,
because the first thing we
saw were the gigantic jaws
of *Carcharodon megalodon*—a
shark that lived 12 million years ago.
"Some size," I said, because this shark was so big it
could have swallowed a whole horse in one gulp.

"Here's another giant," I said. "It's a clam."

Grandma touched the outside of the shell. "It's much rougher than I thought it would be, and it's as hard as a rock!" she said.

"How would you like to see some real rocks?" I asked.

"There are *rocks* in this museum?"

"Not only rocks, but gems and minerals too. Come on, Grandma!"

Grandma knows that I have a rock collection at home. Of course, it's not as big as the museum's. Mine fits inside a shoebox.

I explained that the first rock we looked at wasn't really a rock at all.

"It's a meteorite," I told Grandma. "Meteorites come from outer space."

"How did it get here?" Grandma asked.

"A long time ago it fell to earth
and landed in Greenland," I said.
"Some explorers brought it by ship
all the way to the museum."

Then I took Grandma to see the
geodes, which are stones with scooped-out
holes lined with crystals.

"I love the purple one," Grandma said.

"That's an amethyst geode," I told her.

Personally, I can never decide if my favorite
mineral is malachite, which is green and bubbly looking,
or rhodochrosite, which looks like a tiny red porcupine.
I also like pale blue datolite, and rose-colored quartz. It's
hard to pick a favorite. I could have spent a week there,
but it was time to show Grandma something different.

"I thought you might like to see a few bugs."

"Whatever made you think that?" Grandma asked.

"Because bugs are great," I said, "and we need them on earth just as much as we need ostriches and elephants. Everything helps to balance life in some way."

Grandma bent down and kissed me.

"What's that for?"

"I'm balancing life in my own way," she said. "Now show me your best bug."

"Here it is, Grandma. It's called a goliath beetle. It's four inches long, and its wings are bigger than those of a sparrow."

"I'd certainly be surprised to find one of those in my windowbox," Grandma said.

I told her that would never happen. "Goliath beetles live only in Africa."

"How do you feel about frogs, Grandma?"

"I think I like them. Why?"

"Because frogs are fantastic! We studied them in school to learn about life cycles."

"We did the same thing when *I* was in school," Grandma said. "Some things never change."

"You're wrong, Grandma. Tadpoles change. Hop on over and have a look!"

"Grandma, I think that we should look at the human biology exhibit next. Our teacher told us that when we look at the animal world, we shouldn't forget about the mammals we know best—ourselves."

"I like that idea."

"Our circulatory system looks kind of like a big map with highways and roads and rivers," I told her.

"And I guess good health is all about keeping the roadways clear and not littering," she added. I think Grandma was trying to tell me not to eat junk food, but I already knew I shouldn't do that.

I decided it was time to do something really different, so I asked Grandma if she wanted to do some time traveling.

"Of course," she answered.

"Then bundle up and hold my hand," I said. "We're off to the Ice Age."

The first thing
we saw were
the fossils of
a mammoth.
Each of its huge
curving tusks was
16 feet long!
We looked at a
wall that showed a painting
of what the world might have
looked like when herds of woolly
mammoths and reindeer roamed.
"Just looking at it makes me shiver,"
Grandma said.

Grandma bent down and gave me a hug. "Thank you for a wonderful trip," she said. "Now it's my turn to take you someplace, and the place I'm going to take you is the museum shop."

"You are?"

"This trip with you was like a cake, delicious and sweet. You made the cake, but it takes a grandma to add the icing."

Sometimes my grandma talks in riddles. But that's okay. She bought me a terrific snowflake obsidian for my rock collection. I plan to put it in a very special place in my shoebox.

A few words from Molly about the exhibits

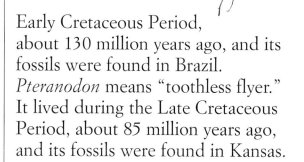

Pages 12–13
Allosaurus (AL-oh-SAWR-us) means "different lizard." It was 35 feet long and had large claws on its feet and hands. *Allosaurus* lived during the Late Jurassic Period, about 140 million years ago. Its fossils were found in Wyoming.

Pages 14–15
Stegosaurus (STEG-oh-SAWR-us) means "spiked lizard." It had a huge, heavy body and a small head with a brain no bigger than a walnut. *Stegosaurus* measured 20 feet long and lived during the Late Jurassic Period, about 140 million years ago. Its fossils were found in Wyoming.

Pages 16–17
Pterosaur (TEHR-oh-sawr) means "winged lizard." *Tupuxuara* means "flying spirit." It lived during the

Early Cretaceous Period, about 130 million years ago, and its fossils were found in Brazil. *Pteranodon* means "toothless flyer." It lived during the Late Cretaceous Period, about 85 million years ago, and its fossils were found in Kansas.

Pages 18–19
Apatosaurus (ah-PAT-oh-SAWR-us) means "deceptive lizard." Weighing over 30 tons, it measured 86 feet long and 14 feet high at the shoulder. *Apatosaurus* may have traveled in herds or family groups, much the way elephants do today. It lived during the Late Jurassic Period, about 140 million years ago. Its fossils were found in Wyoming.

Pages 20–21

Tyrannosaurus rex (tye-RAN-oh-SAWR-us reks) means "tyrant lizard king." *Tyrannosaurus rex* was 40 feet long. It had a large head and deep jaws with large, curved teeth. The largest teeth measured 6 inches in length. *T. rex* lived during the Late Cretaceous Period, about 65 million years ago. Its fossils were found in Montana.

Pages 22–23, 24–25, and 28–29

A diorama (DYE-oh-RAM-uh) is a three-dimensional scene showing figures in a realistic setting, complete with lifelike trees, plants, and backgrounds.

Pages 26–27

African elephants weigh between 7,000 and 13,000 pounds—as much as five station wagons!

Adults stand 8 to 13 feet tall at the shoulder. African savanna elephants have the biggest ears in the world—from top to bottom they measure up to 6 ½ feet.

Pages 30–31

Carcharodon megalodon (kar-KAIR-oh-DON MEG-uh-loh-DON) was 35 to 45 feet long. Megalodon means "big tooth."

Pages 32–33

The Cape York Meteorite hit Greenland about 10,000 years ago. In 1908, Arctic explorer Robert E. Peary brought it to New York City. Estimated to be about 4 ½ billion years old, it measures 10 feet by 8 feet and weighs about 33 tons.

Pages 34–35
The goliath beetle is one of the most famous types of scarab beetle. Children in Africa sometimes catch these giant beetles and fly them around on the end of a string.

Pages 36–37
The reticulated python is 23 feet long, with 321 vertebrae in its body and 91 in its tail.

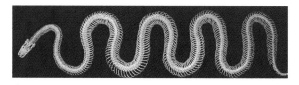

Pages 38–39
The human circulatory system is a network of blood vessels that reach all parts of the body except the hair and nails. The heart acts as a pump to keep the system in motion.

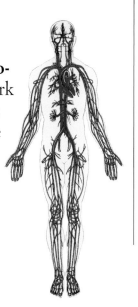

Pages 40–41
Mammoths became extinct about 10,000 years ago. They were about the same size as elephants, but their tusks were much longer and more curved. Their fossils were found in Indiana.

Page 42
Cave bears lived only in Europe from 20,000 to 14,000 years ago. Their fossils were found in caves in the Alps. Prehistoric people also lived in such caves and drew pictures of these bears on cave walls.

A word from Grandma

We are the generation of galloping grandparents. We're off on a trip. We're hurrying to our own events. We are the busiest generation of grandparents ever to pack a suitcase. Still of all the trips we take, none can compare to one with a grandchild.

All of us grandparents know about children from top to bottom; we button tops and change bottoms. We worry over sniffles, and we try to be on hand when we're needed, although we feel that there may be times when the parents of those children we cherish find us too much to handle. Do we expect too much in the way of returned interest, too many hugs and too many hellos?

I was excited and delighted when my darling Molly offered her expertise in traveling a world I rarely visit. What I learned, of course, went beyond the things we saw. As we walked the halls of the museum, I felt totally connected—the connection not only of Molly and me, but the connection of life to life, of the living to the living and the once-alive to the yet-to-be-born.

When we reached the street, I hugged my granddaughter and thanked her.

No, this is not an easy world we share. But what a joy to be alive.

Thank you, Molly, for making me aware of all life.

*The authors wish to thank the American Museum of
Natural History in New York for providing the setting
for our adventure together—and for the considerable
help given by Maron Waxman and Jackie Beckett.*

*Our publishing experience at Workman was made special
by the loving care of our talented and concerned editor,
Michaela Muntean, and her associates, particularly
Nancy Loggins Gonzalez who designed the book.*

*We also thank Robert L. Bernstein who first had
the idea that grandmothers belong in a museum
and so began our project.*